A Desert Scrapbook
Dawn to Dusk in the Sonoran Desert

cactus wren

by Virginia Wright-Frierson

Simon & Schuster
Books for Young Readers

OREGON
IDAHO
GREAT BASIN DESERT
CALIFORNIA
NEVADA
UTAH
CO
MOJAVE DESERT
ARIZONA
SONORAN DESERT
NEW MEXICO
MEXICO
CHIHUAHUAN DESERT

SIMON & SCHUSTER BOOKS FOR YOUNG READERS

An imprint of Simon & Schuster Children's Publishing Division

1230 Avenue of the Americas, New York, New York 10020

Copyright © 1996 by Virginia Wright-Frierson.

SIMON & SCHUSTER BOOKS FOR YOUNG READERS is a trademark of Simon & Schuster.

The text for this book is set in Palatino. The illustrations are rendered in watercolor.

Manufactured in Hong Kong by South China Printing Company (1988) Ltd.

First Edition

10 9 8 7 6 5 4 3 2 1

Library of Congress Cataloging-in-Publication Data

Wright-Frierson, Virginia. A desert scrapbook: dawn to dusk in the Sonoran Desert
by Virginia Wright-Frierson. —1st ed.

p.   cm.

Summary: The author/artist describes many of the animals and plants and their
surroundings that she has sketched in the Sonoran Desert.

1. Desert biology—Sonoran Desert—Juvenile literature. (1. Sonoran Desert. 2. Desert
animals. 3. Desert plants.) I. Title QH104.5.S58W75 1996 95-19629 574.9791'7—dc20

ISBN 0-689-80678-7

*For my husband, Dargan Frierson, whose work first brought us to the
Sonoran Desert, and to our Tucson friends who help us to come back.*

*The author would like to thank Ms. Carol Madeheim, Education Specialist II,
and Dr. Peter Siminski, Curator of Mammology and Ornithology at the
Arizona-Sonora Desert Museum.*

FOR INFORMATION ABOUT EFFORTS TO PRESERVE, EXHIBIT, AND
PROTECT THIS FRAGILE ECOSYSTEM, PLEASE CONTACT:

> The Arizona-Sonora Desert Museum
> 2021 North Kinney Road
> Tucson, AZ 85743

I find a beautiful view and sit quietly, listening and waiting for the animals to get used to my presence. Some people think that our Sonoran Desert is just a dry land of mountains, strange plants, and great sweeping skies. But look very carefully and you will also see many interesting creatures.

Once, on a spring day when I was out painting a prickly pear cactus, a desert tortoise crept up to nibble on a ripe fruit. I quickly sketched it until it crawled away with a red-stained mouth.

prickly pear blossom - May

Another time when I was painting wildflowers, I noticed that a shadow kept passing over my white paper. When I looked up, I was surprised to see a vulture circling right above me. It was so close I could see its wrinkled head and the sunlight through its large wings. It flew off as soon as I waved my arms to show I was not dead and it would not be eating me for lunch.

Today, as I sketch some doves, I am startled by a roadrunner bursting from behind a nearby barrel cactus. It catches a zebra-tailed lizard and dashes off, leaving a little cloud of dust.

barrel cactus bloom - August
(my favorite cactus flower)

cactus wren feather

cactus wrens

A cactus wren emerges from its nest of twigs and dry grasses in a jumping cholla (*CHOY-uh*). I draw many studies of the nest and the mother wren as she flies back and forth with beetle larvae for her babies.

The sun is getting higher and the day is getting hotter. Most of the animals are now resting in cooler, shady places to escape the broiling heat. They will not come out until the cool of evening and the cover of darkness.

A tarantula waits until nightfall in its cool underground tunnel.

A desert pack rat is asleep, curled up deep inside its messy mound of cactus joints, sticks, leaves, bark, and rocks.

A desert scorpion hides under a rock, its babies clustered safely on its back.

A black-tailed jackrabbit rests in a shallow hole it has dug in the shade of a mesquite tree.

An elf owl sleeps in a hole in a saguaro.

A kangaroo rat lies asleep, curled up all day in its deep burrow. They never need to drink water, but get all the moisture they need from seeds and plants gathered at night.

A western diamondback rattlesnake stays cool in the abandoned hole of an antelope squirrel.

saguaro flowers - May

The creamy white flowers of the saguaros (*suh-WAHR-ohs*) have finished blooming for this year, and now the fruit begins to ripen. It is feasted upon by many desert animals, insects, and birds. This gila (*HEE-luh*) woodpecker has a nest in the hole it has pecked in the giant cactus.

Gila woodpecker feather

I rest in the shade of a palo verde tree and look at some seeds and pods I've collected. Above me, a curve-billed thrasher cools itself by widely opening its beak.

This small saguaro is about twenty-five years old!

palo verde pods

mesquite beans

jojoba nut

desert willow pod

creosote bush

prickly pear fruit

catclaw acacia

devil's claw
before the
pod opens–

Saguaro
fruit

This story happened a few years ago: I was sitting on the hot ground painting a mountain view when I noticed a slight movement under a bush. My eyes focused on a huge rattlesnake, coiled and perfectly camouflaged next to my foot! I eased back, trembling, and as the snake slowly moved away, I saw a large lump in its middle. Luckily for me, it must have just eaten a cottontail.

Thunder grumbles in the distance and I notice the air is heavier. Maybe today will bring the first rain of the summer monsoons. The dry stalks of the ocotillo (*ah-ko-TEE-oh*) wave in the hot wind, welcoming the coming storm. I head for my home, looking down as I always do when I walk in the desert, careful not to brush against a spiny cactus or twist an ankle on the loose rock.

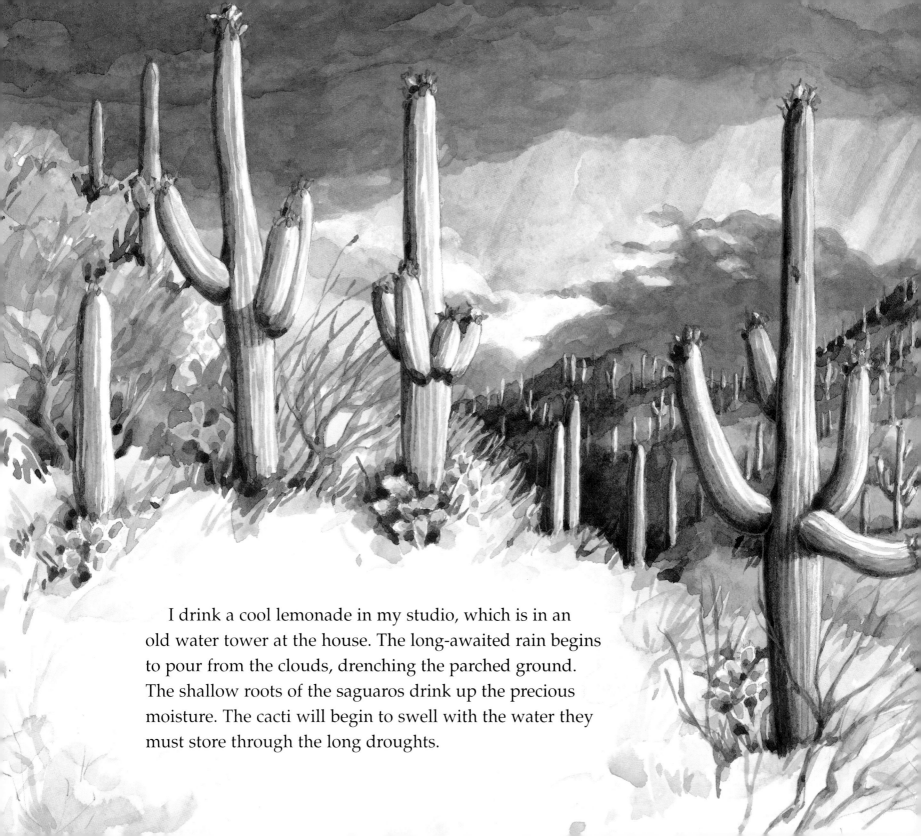

I drink a cool lemonade in my studio, which is in an
old water tower at the house. The long-awaited rain begins
to pour from the clouds, drenching the parched ground.
The shallow roots of the saguaros drink up the precious
moisture. The cacti will begin to swell with the water they
must store through the long droughts.

With a great crashing of thunder, lightning strikes the tallest saguaro on the mountain!

It will collapse and its skeleton will stand with the wooden ribs reaching to the sky like fingers. But the fallen cactus will provide shelter and food for many insects and small animals.

I stay inside until the storm passes, carefully sorting some of the cactus spines I have collected.

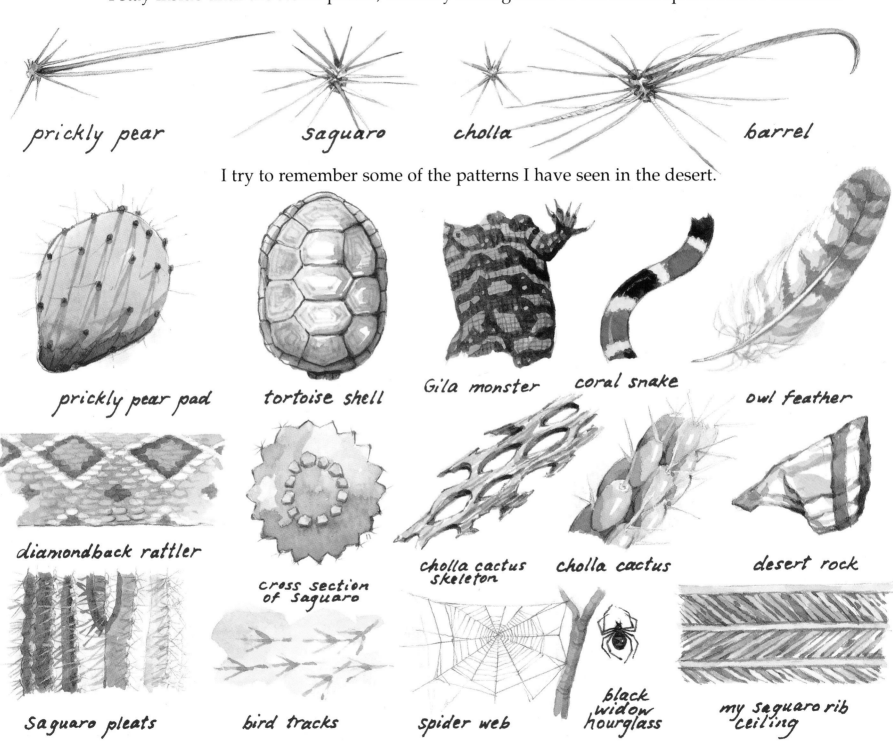

prickly pear   saguaro   cholla   barrel

I try to remember some of the patterns I have seen in the desert.

prickly pear pad   tortoise shell   Gila monster   coral snake   owl feather

diamondback rattler   cross section of saguaro   cholla cactus skeleton   cholla cactus   desert rock

Saguaro pleats   bird tracks   spider web   black widow hourglass   my saguaro rib ceiling

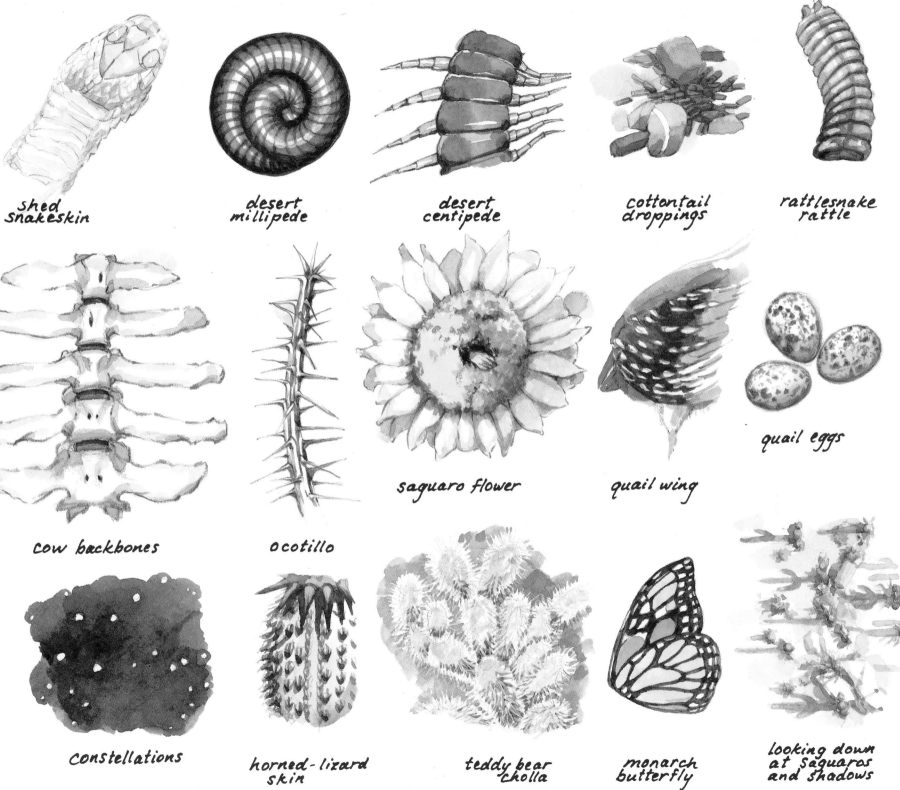

shed
snakeskin

desert
millipede

desert
centipede

cottontail
droppings

rattlesnake
rattle

cow backbones

ocotillo

saguaro flower

quail wing

quail eggs

constellations

horned-lizard
skin

teddy bear
cholla

monarch
butterfly

looking down
at saguaros
and shadows

I love to come outside right after a rain has freshened the
air and settled the dust. I walk to the dry arroyo near my
house and hear a roaring sound.

after

Suddenly, the arroyo is filled with churning water. So much rain falls in such a short time, it cannot all soak into the baked earth. The water collects in many streambeds in the mountains and becomes a muddy, roaring flash flood in the valleys. (Don't ever camp in an arroyo!)

By evening the spadefoot toads that have been buried
deep underground all year have dug up to the surface.
They croak and sing and lay eggs in the muddy pools. The
eggs must develop into tadpoles, and then baby toads,
before the puddles dry up in a few days.

The toads eat many insects in their few days aboveground. Then they dig back underground for almost a year to await another rainy season.

Once I saw several garter snakes feasting on spadefoot tadpoles in a puddle.

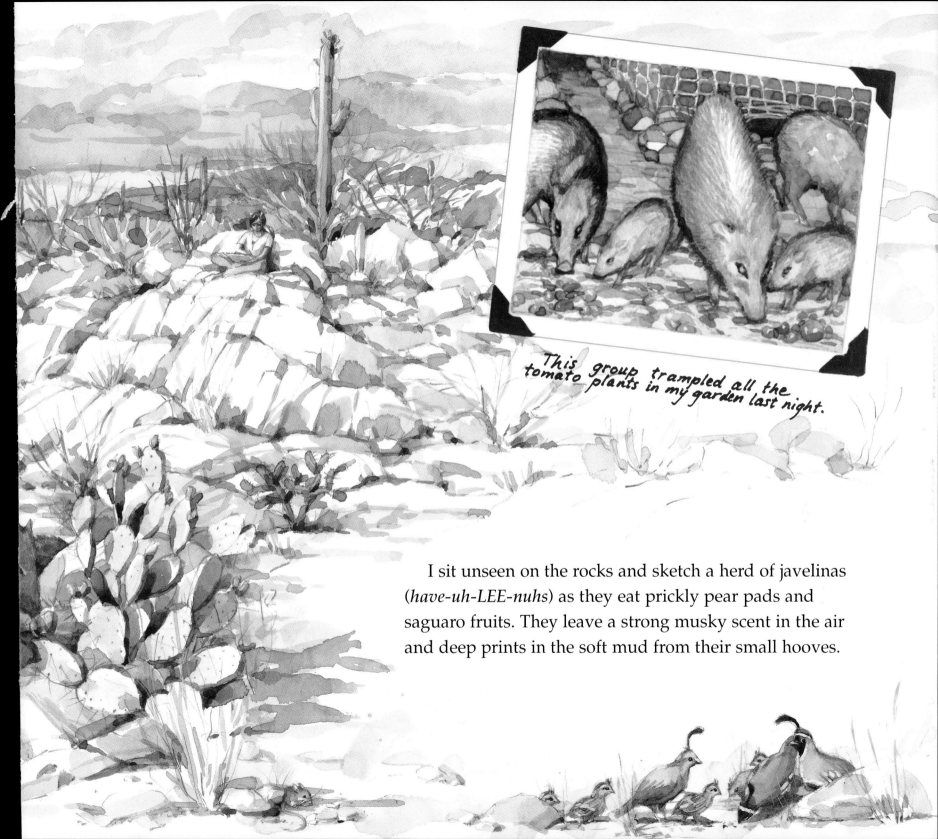

This group trampled all the tomato plants in my garden last night.

I sit unseen on the rocks and sketch a herd of javelinas (*have-uh-LEE-nuhs*) as they eat prickly pear pads and saguaro fruits. They leave a strong musky scent in the air and deep prints in the soft mud from their small hooves.

There is always a glorious sunset after a rainstorm. The pungent smell of the desert creosote bush perfumes the air. I sit on the rocks with my watercolors, trying to capture the warm glowing light and fiery colors.

The desert sky grows dark as I return home. A great horned owl sweeps soundlessly above my head.

The air fills with sounds of life after night falls in the desert. Nocturnal creatures creep out of their tunnels and burrows. I hear an elf owl calling from its hole in a saguaro. The toads croak and sing. Coyotes yip and howl.

In the studio, I spread out my sketches of these Sonoran Desert plants and animals, and the feathers, spines, and seeds I have found. I think maybe I will collect today's work into a scrapbook that will give a feeling of this desert day from dawn to dusk.

Outside my tower window, thousands of bright stars pierce the immense blackness of the beautiful night sky.

white-winged dove   antelope squirrel   desert cottontail   cactus wren   desert tortoise

tarantula hawk

black-vulture

bark scorpion

harvester ants

roadrunner

zebra-tailed lizard

pack rat

tarantula   kangaroo rat   black-tailed jack rabbit   Western diamondback rattlesnake   elf owl   gila woodpecker